The Scarecrows' Wedding

Julia Donaldson

ALISON GREEN BOOKS

Axel Scheffler

Betty O'Barley and Harry O'Hay
Were scarecrows. (They scared
  lots of crows every day.)
Harry loved Betty, and Betty loved Harry,
So Harry said, "Betty, my beauty, let's marry!
Let's have a wedding, the best wedding yet,
A wedding that no one will ever forget."

Betty agreed, so they hugged
and they kissed.
Then Betty said, "Harry, dear,
let's make a list."

"Just as you say," answered Harry O'Hay,
So they wrote down the
   Things they would Need on the Day:

A dress of
white feathers

a necklace
of shells

Lots of
pink flowers

two rings

and some
bells

Then Harry gave Betty O'Barley his arm
And the scarecrows set off on a
   hunt round the farm.

They hadn't gone far when
   they spotted some geese.
"Oh, geese, if you'll give us a feather a-piece,
You can come to our wedding,
   the best wedding yet,
The wedding that no one will ever forget."

"We will," honked the geese, and they each gave a feather.

(A spider friend offered to sew them together.)

"Hooray!" cried the scarecrows.
  They hugged and they kissed,
And they hurried back home
  and crossed "dress" off their list.

Then Harry gave Betty O'Barley his arm,
And they set off once more
  on their hunt round the farm.

They hadn't gone far when some cows gathered round,
And the bells round their necks made a wonderful sound.
Ring-a-ding ding! Ring-a-ding ding!
"Oh, cows, will you please come and make your bells ring
For our wonderful wedding, the best wedding yet,
The wedding that no one will ever forget?"

A dress of
white feathers

a necklace
of shells

Lots of
Pink flowers

two rings

and some
bells

"Yes," mooed the cows. "We can tinkle our bells."

Then a crab scuttled up
with a necklace of shells!

Some mice found two rings
in a bin. (They were certain
The rings had belonged
to an old farmhouse curtain.)

"Hooray!" cried the scarecrows.
  They hugged and they kissed.
"Pink flowers are the only things left on our list."
Then Harry said, "Betty, dear, I can find those.
Why don't I pick some while you have a doze?"

"Pink flowerzzz? Pink flowerzzz?"
  buzzed a big stripy bee.
"I can find you a field of pink flowerzzz!
  Follow me."

So the bee led the way, and they travelled for hours
Till they came to a field full of pretty pink flowers.
Harry stood thinking. "I won't pick them yet.
I'll need to find water, to keep their stalks wet."

"Just follow me,"
   croaked a lumpy old toad.
"There's a lovely wet pool
   at the top of this road."

They climbed up the road.

It was terribly steep.

"I'm tired," said the toad,
so they stopped for a sleep.

Early next morning they came to the pool.
"This water," said Harry, "is beautifully cool,
But now I need something to carry it in –
A jug or a vase or a cup or a tin."

"I think I can help," said a small squirly snail.
"I can show you the way to a very fine pail."

So the snail and the scarecrow
set off on their way,

But the snail was so slow . . .

. . . it took more than a day.

Betty was worried.

"What's happened to Harry?
Where is the scarecrow
I'm planning to marry?"

The farmer came by with a frown on his face,
And he made a new scarecrow to take Harry's place.

"Good day," said the scarecrow. "I'm Reginald Rake."
He took Betty's hand and he gave it a shake.

"Together," he told her, "we make a fine pair.
You're really quite pretty, apart from your hair."
Then he jumped in the tractor and told her, "Hop in.
I'm a really fast driver. Let's go for a spin."

But Betty said, "No – I must wait here for Harry.
He is the scarecrow I'm going to marry.
We're planning our wedding, the best wedding yet,
The wedding that no one will ever forget."

Reginald laughed. "You'll be waiting for ever.
Forget about Harry! I bet he's not clever.

"I must be the cleverest scarecrow alive.
I can sing lots of songs. I can dance, I can drive!
I'm dashing! I'm daring! I'm cool as can be!
I can even blow smoke rings
   – just watch me and see!"

And he took out a big fat cigar from a packet
The farmer had foolishly left in his jacket.
"But smoking is *bad* for you!" Betty exclaimed.
"Really you ought to be feeling ashamed."

"Don't be a fusspot," said Reginald Rake.
"My smoke rings are staggering, make no mistake."
He struck up a light and he tried hard to smoke . . .
But straight away started to splutter and choke.

What happened next was completely unplanned:
The lighted cigar tumbled out of his hand.

It fell to the ground – and it started a fire.
Betty screamed, "Help!"
as the flames flickered higher.

But Reginald Rake said, "I'd better be off,"
And he bounded away with a terrible cough.

Then suddenly,
   who should appear on the farm
But Harry O'Hay,
   with a pail on his arm.

"Betty!" cried Harry. "My own future wife!"
He poured on the water – and saved Betty's life.

Then they picked up the flowers, they hugged and they kissed,

And they said, "Now that's everything crossed off the list."

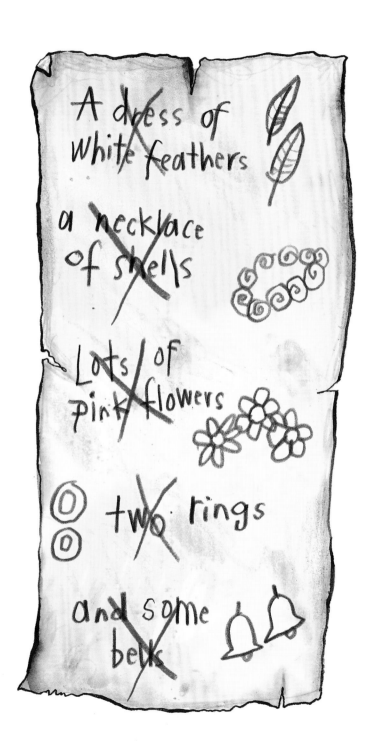

A dress of ~~white~~ feathers

a necklace of ~~shells~~

Lots of ~~pink~~ flowers

~~two~~ rings

and some ~~bells~~

So Betty O'Barley and Harry O'Hay
Wed one another the very next day,
And everyone (even the snail, who was late)
Said, "Don't they look happy?" and, "Don't they look great?"

"This," they agreed, as they sprinkled confetti
On Harry O'Hay and his beautiful Betty,
"Is the best wedding ever, the best wedding yet,
The wedding that no one will ever forget."

For Ally and Chris, and for Jerry and Teresa – J.D.

This edition published in the UK by Alison Green Books, 2023
An imprint of Scholastic
1 London Bridge, London, SE1 9BG
Scholastic Ireland, 89E Lagan Road, Dublin Industrial Estate, Glasnevin, Dublin, D11 HP5F

SCHOLASTIC and associated logos are trademarks and/or
registered trademarks of Scholastic Inc.

First published in the UK by Alison Green Books, 2014

Text © Julia Donaldson, 2014
Illustrations © Axel Scheffler, 2014

The moral rights of Julia Donaldson and Axel Scheffler have been asserted.

ISBN 978 0702 31932 7

A CIP catalogue record for this book is available from the British Library.

Printed in China

Paper made from wood grown in sustainable forests and other controlled sources.

1 3 5 7 9 10 8 6 4 2

www.scholastic.co.uk